# The Midnight Fairies

# PaRragon

Bath · New York · Singapore · Hong Kong · Cologne · Delhi · Melbourne

Megan was staying with Grandma for a few days,
while Mom was away.

Megan always had fun at Grandma's. At the far end
of Grandma's yard there was a big old oak tree with
a swing, where Megan loved to play.

On the second night of Megan's visit, as Grandma helped her get ready for bed, Megan realized that she'd lost her pretty flower necklace. Megan and Grandma looked everywhere, but they couldn't find it.

Megan began to cry. "Mom gave me that necklace," she said tearfully. "It's really special."

Grandma gave Megan a hug. "Don't worry. We'll look in the yard tomorrow," she promised. "I'm sure it will be there."

Megan settled down to sleep, but she tossed and turned and finally woke up again. She couldn't stop thinking about her lost necklace.

Getting out of bed, she went to look out at the yard, where she hoped she might see it.

Somewhere in the distance, a clock chimed once...

twice...twelve times. "Midnight!" Megan thought.

Suddenly, Megan's eyes opened wide. At the end of the moonlit

yard, where the wildflowers grew, lights began to wink and

twinkle, and shimmering shapes seemed to dance in the air.

Fairies had come out to play!
There was Firefly, a little red-haired fairy...

Moon Blossom, a fairy with
hair like finely spun silk...

Nightingale, a
fairy with cheeks
like rose petals...

and Stardust, a fairy with
glimmering pink wings.

Together, the four fairies danced and skipped through the air, laughing as they flitted from flower to flower.

All at once Firefly spotted something—
a silver necklace gleaming in the grass.

"Look!" she said to her friends.

"I wonder who this belongs to!"

"Maybe it's that little girl's," said Nightingale, pointing up
to the window where Megan was looking out. "She looks very sad—
as if she's lost something special."

"I wish we could make her smile again," said Moon Blossom.

The fairies looked at one another, and knew they were all thinking the same thing. First, they tucked the necklace safely behind a stone. Then, together, they flew across the yard and straight up to Megan's window.

As Megan gasped with amazement and delight,

Stardust sprinkled her with glittering fairy dust.

"Now you'll be able to fly with us!" the fairies said happily.

With a fairy holding each hand,
Megan whooshed out of the window and
flew down to the far end of the yard.

When they landed, Stardust introduced herself and her friends. "We are the Midnight Fairies," she explained. "Every night at midnight, we come out to dance and play in the moonlight. Will you be our friend and play with us tonight?"

"Of course I will!" said Megan happily.

With the moon beaming down and the friendly stars twinkling above, Megan and the fairies danced among the wildflowers.

The cool grass tickled Megan's toes, and the fairies'
laughter sounded like tiny crystal bells. Megan laughed
with them, and felt happier than she ever had before.

When Megan was too tired to dance anymore,
Firefly said, "We have a surprise for you."
And she brought out Megan's silver necklace.
"My necklace!" cried Megan. "You found it!
Oh, thank you!"

As Firefly gave the necklace
back, Stardust sprinkled magic fairy
dust over it. A beautiful fairy
appeared in place of the flower.

"Oh!" breathed Megan. "It's
you! It's a Midnight Fairy!"

"Yes," said Firefly. "But please
don't tell anyone how it got there,
or we might lose our magic."

"I promise!" replied Megan.

As she put on her necklace, Megan realized that she could barely keep her eyes open. With the Midnight Fairies fluttering over her, she curled up under the oak tree and fell asleep until... the morning, when she woke up, tucked into her cozy bed in Grandma's house!

"How did I get back here?"
Megan wondered. "Was it just a dream?"

She reached up to her neck—and
there was her necklace, right
where it should be.

"Hello!" said Grandma cheerfully,
opening the bedroom door.

"Grandma, look!" said Megan. "I have
my necklace back! Did YOU find it?"

"No, dear," said Grandma, with a puzzled look. She peered down at the necklace. "Oh, how lovely!" she said. "I hadn't noticed the fairy before."

"The Midnight Fairies!" Megan thought to herself. "So it wasn't a dream, after all!"

"I wonder how your necklace got back
here," said Grandma, scratching her head.
Megan, smiling as she looked out
toward the yard, knew the answer.

But it was a secret that belonged
to her—to her and the Midnight
Fairies, the wonderful, magical
friends she would never, ever forget.

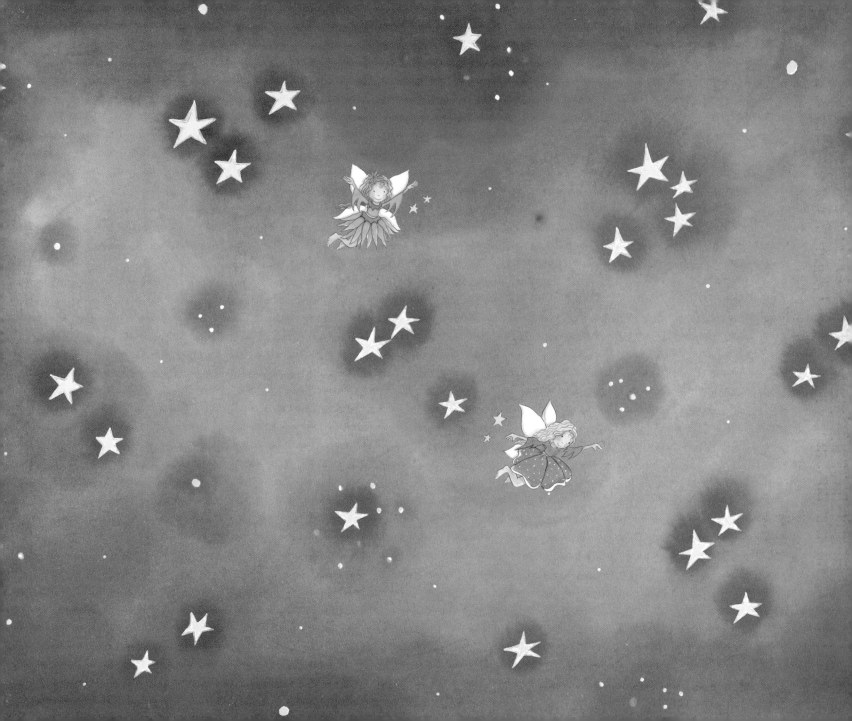